A ROOKIE READER®

LISTEN TO ME

By Barbara J. Neasi

Illustrations by Gene Sharp

Prepared under the direction of Robert Hillerich, Ph.D.

CHILDRENS PRESS®

CHICAGO

For my mother, Florence

Library of Congress Cataloging in Publication Data

Neasi, Barbara J.
  Listen to me.

  (A Rookie Reader)
  Summary: Whenever Mom and Dad are too busy to
talk and to listen, Grandma saves the day, helping out
and being a good listener.
  [1. Grandmothers—Fiction. 2. Listening—Fiction]
I. Title. II. Series.
PZ7.N295Li 1986   [E]   86-10664
ISBN 0-516-02072-2

13 14 15 16 17 18 R 02 01 00 99 98

I like to ask questions.

I like to hear stories.

Sometimes Mom is too busy
to listen to me.

Sometimes Dad is too busy
to talk to me.

That's when I need Grandma.

When Grandma takes me shopping,

she listens to me.

When I take Grandma for a walk,

I listen to her.

When Grandma drives
me to dance class, she listens
to me.

15

When I take Grandma to lunch,

I listen to her.

19

When Grandma helps
me draw pictures, she listens
to me.

When I help Grandma pull weeds,

I listen to her.

Sometimes Grandma and I
sit in the yard,

we talk and listen together.

30

Grandma says, "Everyone needs a good listener."

WORD LIST

a	Grandma	Mom	talk
and	hear	need(s)	that's
ask	help(s)	pictures	the
busy	her	pull	to
class	I	questions	together
Dad	in	says	too
dance	is	she	walk
draw	like	shopping	we
drives	listen(s)	sit	weeds
everyone	listener	sometimes	when
for	lunch	stories	yard
good	me	take(s)	

About the Author

Barbara Neasi is a writer and the mother of twin daughters. She wrote her first book, *Just Like Me*, because she found there was a lack of suitable material describing how twins can look the same and like the same things, but in many other ways they are very different. In *Listen to Me*, the second book she has published with Childrens Press, Mrs. Neasi explores the wonderful relationship a young boy has listening to and sharing things with his grandmother.

About the Artist

Gene Sharp was born and grew up in Iowa. He lives and works as an artist in the Chicago area. He has illustrated several of the Rookie Readers including *Too Many Balloons* and *Purple Is Part of a Rainbow*.